# PETER PUCK
### and the
## Runaway Zamboni® Machine

# PETER PUCK

## and the

## Runaway Zamboni® Machine

**BRIAN MCFARLANE**
*illustrated by* **GERI STOREY**

FENN
TUNDRA

Published in Canada by Fenn/Tundra of Tundra Books,
a division of Random House of Canada Limited
One Toronto Street, Suite 300, Toronto, Ontario M5C 2V6

Published in the United States by Fenn/Tundra Tundra Books of Northern New York,
P.O. Box 1030, Plattsburgh, New York 12901

Library of Congress Control Number: 2013953677

Library and Archives Canada Cataloguing in Publication

McFarlane, Brian, 1931–, author
Peter Puck and the runaway Zamboni / by Brian McFarlane
; illustrated by Geri Storey.

(The adventures of hockey's greatest mascot)
ISBN 978-1-77049-583-8 (bound)

I. Storey, Geri, illustrator  II. Title.

PS8575.F37P467 2014        jC813'.54        C2013-906928-3

ZAMBONI and the configuration of the Zamboni® ice resurfacing machine
are registered in the U.S. Patents and Trademark Office as the trademarks of
Frank J. Zamboni & Co., Inc.

Edited by Debbie Rogosin
The text was set in Fairfield.
www.randomhouse.ca

Printed and bound in China

1 2 3 4 5 6        19 18 17 16 15 14

# Contents

## CHAPTER 1

# Game Day!

*P*eter Puck jumped out of the freezer and shook his little rubber body, sending bits of ice flying in all directions.

"Brrr," said Peter. "I'm colder than a polar bear's nose. It's time to warm up with my morning skate."

Moments later, Peter was gliding around the home arena of the Bay City Bobcats hockey team. The huge rink was all his. By evening it would be jammed with screaming fans. Tonight the Bobcats were hosting the Beantown Bruins in a late-season game. The winning team would be in the playoffs.

Peter's tiny skates made soft, crunching sounds as he gathered speed.

"Skating is a really good waker-upper," he always told his friends. "And when you've just spent several hours in the freezer, you need a good waker-upper."

Peter didn't mind sleeping in the freezer. He knew it was important for pucks to be kept frozen before games. It made them less bouncy when players slapped them around the ice.

Peter was the most famous hockey puck of them all, and he loved his job. Nothing was more exciting than being on the ice in the thick of the action of a hockey game.

Peter's thoughts were interrupted by a rumbling at the far end of the arena. It was the Zamboni Ice Resurfacing Machine. Tony Zamboni was Peter's good friend, and he was

3

making his first run of the day.

Tony's engine purred softly as he began to circle the ice.

"Go, Tony, go!" shouted Peter. He scooted out of Tony's way.

Tony beeped his horn twice. It was his way of saying, "Good morning, Peter."

When Tony's work was done, Peter skated over. "Tony!" he shouted. "Where's your partner? The rules call for two Zambonis to create new ice."

"You mean Zack? He had the hiccups last night. He scooped up something that didn't agree with him. I may have to work alone tonight."

"Well, you've done it before. I just hope you don't get sick or we're in big trouble. You do a very important job. The players and fans rely on you, Tony."

Tony sighed. "I'm never part of the action like you are, Pete. My job is boring. Even the new horn I got for my birthday didn't make me happy."

"Gee, I'm sorry to hear that, Tony," Peter said. "Is there anything I can do? I could change your sparkplugs or add a little oil to your crankcase."

"Oh, it's nothing like that, Pete. I just get tired of doing the same thing every day. Getting filled with water. Always circling the arena clockwise. Needing more water. And getting shooed off so that others can play on my ice."

"Be careful what you wish for, Tony," Peter said. "Would you rather be a garbage truck?"

Tony chuckled. "No, no. Garbage trucks are smelly, and I'd rather be full of water than garbage. Still, there's more to life than

making circles around a hockey rink. I never
even get to go outside."

Peter tried to cheer up his friend.

"Tony, I'm sorry you feel that way. Just
remember, you're a VIZ around here."

"What's that?"

"A Very Important Zamboni."

"Thanks, Pete. I appreciate that. By the way, I thought it was VIP, not VIZ."

Peter laughed. "VIP stands for something else, Tony."

"Like what?"

"Like, Very Important Puck." He pointed at his chest. "And that would be me."

Tony smiled. "Thanks, Pete. You sure know how to make a fellow feel better."

Tony Zamboni beeped his horn twice and drove off the ice.

Later that morning, Peter was sitting in the referees' dressing room when his friend George Phair came in. George was a big league referee. His nickname was "Always" Phair because he was known for getting things right.

"Hi, Pete. It's good to see you. Resting up for the big game tonight?"

"Yes. It's going to be a thriller."

"I've been out on the rink," said George. "Loosening up a bit. But the ice was all cut up."

"That's odd," said Peter.

The referee began to unlace his skates. "Tony Zamboni always makes fresh ice after the teams take their morning skate. He didn't do that today."

"Did you ask him why not?" Peter asked.

"I couldn't find him," George replied.

Peter jumped off the bench and tugged on the referee's pant leg. "Let's go look for him. I've got a feeling something has happened to Tony."

The first place they checked was Tony's normal parking place. But Tony wasn't there.

Then Peter noticed tire tracks leading to a large door that opened onto the back parking lot.

"Look, George! He's left the building. Tony never does that. I wonder where he went?"

George was surprised, too. "I don't know, Pete, but we can't play a game here tonight if the ice is chipped and slushy."

"We've got to find him, George."

"You're right," said the referee. "I'll get my car."

## CHAPTER 2

# Looking for Adventure

Tony Zamboni had never seen such wonderful sights. He rolled down Bay City's main street, his engine purring and his headlights shining on one interesting thing after another.

Every so often he beeped his horn. People

pointed and laughed. When he passed a school bus, the kids on board waved and cheered. They'd never seen a Zamboni outside.

Being on the road was exciting! When cars and trucks and bicycles raced toward Tony, he beeped his horn, signaling them to get out of his way. When a light changed from green to red, cars in front of him stopped. He slammed on his brakes just in time.

While he was stopped, a man in a convertible pulled up. He glanced at the sky.

"Looks like rain," he said to Tony. "I think I'll put the top up." The man touched a lever and the roof unfolded.

"Good idea, Mister," Tony said. "I'd put my top up, too, but I don't have one. I don't have windshield wipers, either."

The man laughed, and when the light

turned green, he raced away.

Tony drove on, looking for excitement and adventure. He was never going back to the arena.

Ahead he saw a group of men in hard hats. There was smelly black asphalt on the road, and a sturdy paving machine was packing it down. It went back and forth and back and forth over the hot asphalt.

It's almost as smooth as the ice I make, Tony thought. But that machine reminds me of my dull life.

He kept on going.

Then Tony saw a moving van backed up in a driveway. Men were loading furniture into it. Hmmm, thought Tony. I don't think I'd like to be a moving van. Too many heavy things to carry. Too much waiting around.

He kept on going.

Soon Tony found himself at the outskirts of the city. In a parking lot, there was a merry-go-round. Kids were riding around and around on the painted horses. They're going in circles, Tony snorted, just like I do all day.

He kept on going.

Then he heard the roar of powerful engines. Tony hurried toward the sound.

There, in a huge field, was an oval track and a grandstand. It was an auto speedway! Cars zipped around the track. Engines whined and roared.

Oh, boy, Tony thought. This is amazing. My engine could roar like that, given a chance. And my tires hold fast to the ice, so I'm sure they'd hold tight to the racetrack.

Tony drove up to the entrance. A sign hanging next to the gate said:

**BAY CITY MOTOR SPEEDWAY**
SPECIAL RACE TODAY
ANYTHING GOES
OPEN TO ALL VEHICLES AND DRIVERS
BIG CASH PRIZE TO THE WINNER

This was Tony's big chance to be part of the action!

Tony drove through the gates and straight to the starting line. The two men selling tickets looked surprised. Spectators in the grandstand laughed and cheered when Tony chugged into place. Tony beeped his horn.

One of the officials hurried over. "You don't belong here," he said. "Scram."

"No," Tony said stubbornly. "I want to be in the race."

"That's impossible," the man said, growing red in the face. "You're not a race car. You're a Zamboni. Zambonis can't compete."

"That's not what the sign says," Tony replied. "It says the race is open to all vehicles. And I'm a vehicle."

"Listen to me." The man came closer. "There are only two other drivers in this race

– Nasty Ned Doolittle and Dangerous Dan Fogarty. No one else will race against them because Ned and Dan will do anything to win. They play rough."

"I'll take my chances. They don't scare me."

The two drivers were leaning on their cars. They looked mean. The one with the number 10 on his jacket shouted, "Let the big lug in. He'll be glad to get back to his hockey rink when we finish with him."

The other driver growled, "Go home, kid, before your pretty paint job gets messed up."

Tony refused to move.

The red-faced official finally gave in. "Okay, you can race," he said. "Who's going to drive you?"

"I need a driver?" Tony asked.

"Of course. Those are the rules."

There were some mechanics standing nearby.

"Will one of you drive me in the race? Please?" Tony pleaded.

"You must be kidding," one of them replied. "Nobody stands a chance against those two."

Tony was crushed. It was his big chance, and he was going to miss it. He felt like all the air had leaked out of his tires.

## CHAPTER 3

# *The Race Is On!*

**S**uddenly there was a commotion in the crowd. A familiar voice demanded, "Let us through, please." Tony blinked in surprise. There were Peter Puck and George Phair, pushing their way toward him.

"We found you," shouted Peter as he

jumped up into the driver's seat. "Tony, what are you doing here? Why did you run away?"

"Oh, Pete, I didn't mean to upset anybody," Tony replied. "I just wanted some adventure. That's why I want to enter this race."

"But you're not a racer, Tony. You can't win against two old pros."

"I can if you help me, Pete. Be a pal. Be my driver."

Peter realized it was useless to argue with his friend.

The starter raised his flag. The other drivers revved their engines.

"Okay, Tony, I'll drive. But remember, I'm a hockey puck, not a race driver. And after the race, you can do what you want, but I'm heading back to the arena."

The starter waved his flag, and the race was on!

Peter Puck stomped on the gas pedal. Tony Zamboni lurched forward, but Nasty Ned and Dangerous Dan were already in the lead.

"Hey, this is fun," shouted Tony over the roar of the engines. "I never knew I could move so fast."

"You're fast, but not fast enough," yelled Peter. "We'll never catch up."

But they did catch up, because the other drivers slowed down. Before the race, Nasty Ned and Dangerous Dan had made a plan. They would have some fun with Peter and Tony and frighten them so badly they'd quit and go home. Then it would be a two-car race. But even that would be a sham. They'd secretly agreed to finish at the same time, so they could share the prize money.

"I smell trouble, Tony," Peter said. "Why would they let us catch up?"

He knew in a moment. Nasty Ned and Dangerous Dan took turns speeding toward the Zamboni. Just before they smashed into him they pulled away, laughing like hyenas.

"Yikes!" shouted Peter. "That was close."

"I thought we were goners," shrieked Tony, tooting his horn. But he drove steadily on.

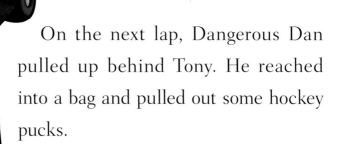

On the next lap, Dangerous Dan pulled up behind Tony. He reached into a bag and pulled out some hockey pucks.

Peter was alarmed. "Tony, he's going to try to knock me off the seat."

"Then he's in for a surprise," Tony answered. "Pete, there's an old goalie mask next to the seat. I found it at the rink this morning. Put it on and be quick about it."

Peter snatched up the mask and pulled it on. It covered his entire body. And just in time. Hockey pucks bounced off the goalie mask, but Peter stayed put.

When Dangerous Dan moved ahead, Tony lurched forward and scraped paint off the back of his car. Dan howled in anger.

"Good move, Tony," shouted Peter.

Then Nasty Ned drove right in front of the Zamboni. In his big fist he clutched a stick of dynamite. And the fuse was lit!

"He's going to throw it," shouted Peter. "He wants to blow us up!"

"Pull that big lever on your right," ordered Tony. "It will lower my conditioner. With any luck, I'll vacuum up the dynamite."

The plan worked. When Nasty Ned tossed the stick of dynamite, it rolled between Tony's wheels and was gobbled up. Peter could hear it rattling around in Tony's huge body, where all the water made the fuse fizzle.

Nasty Ned turned to watch the Zamboni go ka-boom! But nothing happened.

Before Nasty Ned could turn back, Tony Zamboni was charging at him at breakneck speed.

Crash!

Tony's sturdy front end smashed into Nasty Ned's car. The race car flipped over twice and came to a stop. Nasty Ned scrambled out and shook his fist.

"Only one lap to go, Pete," Tony called out. "And one guy left to beat. Where is he, anyway?"

"He's right behind us," Peter answered. "And I'm worried. If he rams us, I'll go flying. I don't have a seat belt."

Then Peter had an idea. "Listen, Tony. Have you got lots of water inside you?"

"I think so, Pete. Pull the small lever. We'll flood him out!"

Peter gave the lever a yank, and a wave of water spread out behind the Zamboni.

Dangerous Dan was so surprised he turned the wheel hard. His car skidded, barreled through a fence, and soared into a

pond. Dangerous Dan waded to shore, a huge
scowl on his face.

Peter Puck chuckled and waved.

The finish line was straight ahead. Peter
grabbed the checkered flag and held it high.
He and Tony had won the big race and the
cash prize! The folks in the grandstand
clapped and cheered.

## CHAPTER 4

# Tony's Big Decision

It had been an amazing day. Now Peter and Tony were on their way back to the Bay City Arena, tired but happy. The race was over, and they were obeying all the speed limits. George Phair had gone ahead to warm up and have his pre-game meal. He wondered

if he'd ever see Tony again. Peter was content
to spend a little more time with his friend
before having to say good-bye.

Tony and Peter passed the merry-go-
round.

"If those were real horses, they'd be
walking in a circle forever," observed Tony.
"They'd see the same sights over and over."

"I see goals scored over and over," said
Peter, "and every one is different."

They passed the moving van, now fully loaded and ready to go.

"I'm glad I'm not a moving van," murmured Tony. "Having furniture bouncing around inside you all the time can't feel very good."

Peter laughed. "It might feel better than having water and a stick of dynamite sloshing around inside you, my friend."

Tony burped.

They passed the paving machine, fast asleep after a long day's work.

"Poor guy," Tony said. "That job can't be much fun."

"Oh, I don't know," replied Peter. "He might enjoy his work. Look how smooth the asphalt is where he rolled it. Cars and trucks and bikes must love driving over it."

"You're right, Pete. Just like hockey players love skating on my smooth ice."

As they approached the arena, Peter gave his friend a pat. "Thanks, Tony, for getting me back in time for the big game. Wherever you go, I wish you luck. Bay City Arena won't be the same without you."

"Hold on, Pete," Tony replied. "I'm not going anywhere."

"But you said . . . "

"Oh, I know. But that was just talk. I'm going back to the arena, and I'm going to stay. That's where I belong. I learned an important lesson today. Each of us has a place in life. I've never been so proud of what I do. I'm no more cut out to be a racing car than that paving machine is meant to make ice."

"But you won the race, Tony. You won big money."

"No, *we* won it, Pete. We're a team. And it was fun. But I don't need the money."

"Well, there are people who do. Let's give it to charity," Peter suggested.

"Great idea," said Tony. And it was settled.

Back at the arena, a crowd had gathered. The coach of the Bobcats called, "We really missed you today, Tony. We need fast ice for the game tonight, and we were afraid you weren't coming back."

"I love you, Tony," a small boy cried. "You are so cool. Too bad you got dented."

"See how much people care about you, Tony," Peter said, beaming. "Come on, let's get ready for the game."

That night, the Bay City Arena was jammed with fans.

Fifteen minutes before the game, the doors parted at the north end of the arena. The lights dimmed and a huge spotlight shone on Tony Zamboni. He was freshly washed and looked splendid!

Peter Puck took a microphone and skated out on the ice.

"Ladies and gentlemen," he began, his voice booming through the building. "From time to time it's important to recognize the men and women and even the machines that help make hockey the grandest team game in the world. Here in Bay City we have an amazing ice-resurfacer. Tonight, let's show him our appreciation. Let's hear it for Tony Zamboni!"

Music blared. The fans rose to their feet, clapping and cheering as Tony glided slowly onto the ice. He blinked his lights and beeped his horn. Then Tony made his first turn around the ice. He scooped up scrapings of snow and ice left from the warm-up. He released exactly the right amount of water, which quickly froze into slick, shiny ice. He had never felt so happy, or so much at home.

The applause continued until Tony finished and headed off, his horn still beeping.

Peter skated back out and took a twirl at center ice. "Folks," he announced, "this ice is perfect! Now, let's play hockey!

# Join Peter on his next adventure!

The Adventures of Hockey's Greatest Mascot

# PETER PUCK

and the **Stolen Stanley Cup**

**BRIAN McFARLANE**

illustrated by **GERI STOREY**